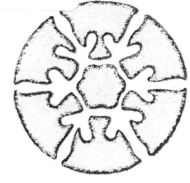

My Brother Loved
SNOWFLAKES

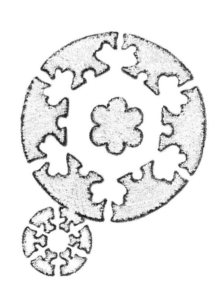

My Brother Loved
SNOWFLAKES

The Story of Wilson A. Bentley, the Snowflake Man

by **Mary Bahr**
Illustrated by **Laura Jacobsen**

For my husband, sons & daughters,
The Jericho Historical Society, and America

M. B.

For Craig and Rugby

L. J.

Text copyright © 2002 by Mary Bahr Fritts
Illustrations copyright © 2002 by Laura Jacobsen

Published by Boyds Mills Press, Inc.
A Highlights Company
815 Church Street
Honesdale, Pennsylvania 18431
Printed in China
Visit our Web site at www.boydsmillspress.com

Publisher Cataloging-in-Publication Data

Fritts, Mary Bahr.
My brother loved snowflakes : the story of Wilson A.
Bentley, the Snowflake Man / by Mary Bahr Fritts ;
illustrated by Laura Jacobsen. —1st ed.

[32] p. : col. ill. ;   cm.
Summary: In this imaginary reminiscence, Charles Bentley recalls the life and times of his
brother, Wilson A. Bentley, who made the study of snow his life's work.
ISBN 1-56397-689-7
1. Bentley, W. A. (Wilson Alwyn), 1865-1931 — Juvenile literature.
2. Snowflakes — Juvenile literature.
3. Meteorologists — United States — Biography — Juvenile literature.
4. Photographers — United States — Biography — Juvenile literature.
(1. Bentley, W. A. (Wilson Alwyn), 1865-1931.
2. Snowflakes. 3. Meteorologists —
United States — Biography.
4. Photographers — United
States — Biography.)
I. Jacobsen, Laura.
II. Title.
551.5/ 092 B 21   CIP
QC858.B46.F75 2002
2001096393

First edition, 2002
The text of this book is set in 14-point Wilke Roman.

10 9 8 7 6 5 4 3 2 1

"A snowflake . . . is a bit of beauty dropped from the sky . . .
that, if lost at that moment, is lost forever to the world."
—W. A. Bentley

SNOWFLAKES LIKED MY BROTHER, WILLIE.
And why not? Nobody cared about them the way he did.
    For Willie, winter couldn't come soon enough. Snow filled
his life like cow's milk fills a bucket.
    "Willie loves water like any other farmer," Mother
explained to visitors. "He just favors it frozen and falling."

But Willie's story doesn't start with snowflakes.
It all began in the green of a Vermont summer.
Willie and I were just boys, chasing up and down
Bentley Lane.

Mother was our teacher. Willie was her best student.
She gave him the love of learning. Then she gave him
the microscope.

I remember how she cradled the wooden box, like it was newborn. The microscope inside was old, but Willie didn't care. Fact is, I never saw him grin so big.

Straightaway, Willie ran outside. He yanked up a
handful of grass and squeezed it under the lens.
"Look, Charlie," he hollered at me. "It's got veins!"

Then he raced to the garden for a flower, to the field for a feather, to Crystal Hill for a stone.

Everything looked new under that microscope. Willie couldn't wait to see it all. But it was a drop of water that changed his life forever.

One sizzler of an afternoon we were fishing Mill Brook.
Nothing much was biting, but I finally caught a little brook
trout. "I'm going to learn everything about it!" Willie shouted.
  I thought he meant to study my fish. But Willie was squinting
through the little glass hole at a splash of water. Water! I never
saw anybody at a fishing hole get so excited about something
that wasn't a fish.

Between milking and playing, music and haying, Willie studied water. I doubt he went a day without staring at some kind of water through his microscope—pond or stream, fog or dew.

And rain! When thunderstorms showered the farm, Willie watched from beginning to end. He even tried to figure out which raindrops came from which cloud.

Then came November. Willie's precious water froze.

"Snow, Charlie. Snow!" Willie shook me awake the morning snow piles buried the farm. I grabbed my sled. Willie grabbed his microscope.

Up on the hill, Willie hunkered down in the snowbank.

"If they're pretty in a pile, imagine what they look like one at a time."

Willie marched out to the meadow. Sitting in a snowdrift, he watched the sky and waited. Sure enough, the clouds hurled a storm.

Willie stood and faced those blizzard winds.
Holding his mittens out like he was carrying a turkey
platter, he reached into the snow swirls for a
snowflake. Just one. Pulling it close to his chest,
he stared at it.

"Hey, Charlie!" he yelled. "Wait'll you see this one!"
By the time I got there, it was gone. Melted. But that
didn't stop Willie. He just grabbed the sky for another.
And another.

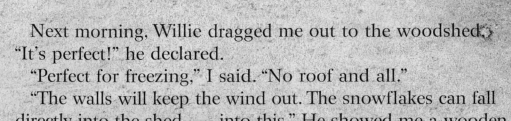

Next morning, Willie dragged me out to the woodshed.
"It's perfect!" he declared.

"Perfect for freezing," I said. "No roof and all."

"The walls will keep the wind out. The snowflakes can fall
directly into the shed . . . into this." He showed me a wooden
tray. "Then I'll put them under the microscope and draw
them before they melt."

"What for?"

"For people to see, Charlie. They're beautiful."

I helped him build a barreltable in a shed with no roof. Mother gave him a black velvet quilting scrap for his tray,
to show off the white of the snowflakes.

It worked. Each crystal sparkled like a jewel. Each one had six matching sides. Each one was as fragile as dragonfly wings.

Willie worked all winter to draw seventy snowflakes. Half the time, the snow crystals melted before he could finish his design. Other times, his fingers were so cold they couldn't hold a pencil.

"Must be a better way," he'd mumble. If there was, I knew Willie would find it.

He did, too. But it took him three whole winters.

One night we were Christmas-wishing from a catalog.

"There's my answer." Willie pointed to a picture. "That camera works with a microscope."

When Father heard the price, he nearly fell off the chair. That usually meant "No!"

Mother just smiled. That usually meant "Somehow." The teacher in her wasn't likely to let anything stand between Willie and learning. Not even a hundred dollars.

But Christmas came and we got overcoats.

Willie's birthday came in February. We had a farmhouse full of food, friends, and favorite songs. Willie and I took turns playing on the piano and clarinet.

I remember how the voices suddenly hushed during "Rock of Ages." Willie's fingers stopped. All eyes turned as Father came through the door carrying one more package. It was a big one.

I think there were tears in Willie's eyes before he tore off the wrapping. He knew how hard it was to squeeze a hundred dollars out of ten dairy cows.

Willie set up his camera in the woodroom
behind the kitchen. But the camera didn't solve all
of his problems.

He couldn't reach the bellows with his short arms.
His warm breath melted the snowflakes.
The turkey feather he used to sweep snow
crystals onto his slides broke some of them.
But *quit* wasn't a Willie word.

He rigged up a string and pulley so he could work the camera. He held his breath while he drew, and moved the snow crystals around with a tiny wooden rod.

I remember the day Willie took his first perfect picture. He yelled so loud, Mother dropped the chicken she was fixing into the flour bin. "We knew you could do it, son," she said, as she wiped flour off her face.

I was glad she said something, because Father just scratched his head. He couldn't see the sense of it all. Nobody seemed interested in snowflakes. Nobody.

Willie's picture of a snowflake was the first one ever. Even I didn't know what to make of it. But I had to admit it was pretty.

After Father died, Willie and I worked the farm up to twenty cows. After chores, Willie stood in the nighttime cold to photograph the northern lights. Or he stood in the pelting rain to capture raindrops in a pan of flour. After they dried, he measured the flour pellets. That way he learned the size of each raindrop.

Besides all that, Willie wrote music for our brass band. He played the church organ. He made animal sounds on his violin for the kids in town.

Meantime, my wife, May, and I grew a family—Alric, Agnus, Arthur, Alice, Archie, Amy, Anna, and Alwyn.

Everybody's kids, not just ours, called him Uncle Willie. They loved his jokes and his music. But most adults just looked at him funny when he talked about snowflakes.

"I guess they think I'm crazy or a fool or both," he said. I saw how it made him sad.

Then he got an idea. "I'll show my slides at the school-house. When people see how beautiful the snowflakes are, they'll understand."

Only six people came.

Willie went right back to his darkroom under the stairs. He photographed everything frozen—rime and sleet, glaze and hail, ice flowers, and frost on windowpanes. He even took pictures of snowrollers, those great big snowballs made by the wind.

Like I said, *quit* wasn't a Willie word.

A college professor named Perkins asked Willie to write about his work. Willie wasn't sure anybody'd want to read about water. But magazines published his articles about snow, rain, clouds, and weather. Before long, dictionaries asked to use his pictures of snowflakes. Colleges wanted to buy them. Greeting card companies put Willie's pictures on their cards. People started calling Willie "the Snowflake Man."

Best of all, scientists who believed in him helped Willie publish a book full of his pictures. He called it *Snow Crystals*.

Finally, everybody could admire the beauty of Willie's snowflakes.

Me? If you ask me what I admired about my brother, I'll tell you a story that has nothing to do with snowflakes.

It was before-the-sun early when I heard the screen door squeak. I spied Willie sneaking out with his camera.

I followed barefoot, without making a sound. The grass was slippery with dew.

Willie crouched next to a tipped-over bucket he'd painted black on the inside. In front of the bucket, I saw a huge grasshopper on a large leaf. The hopper was dripping with dew, like it was wearing pearls.

It didn't move. I couldn't figure out why. Willie took some pictures. Still, it still didn't fly away.

I stretched my neck until I could see why. The hopper was tied to the leaf with Mother's sewing thread.

"There, there," Willie said, whisper-like. "One snip and you're free." He cut the thread and waited til the hopper flew. Then he headed back to the barn.

I laid in the grass for a long while.

That's the way I'll remember my brother. Always seeing the beauty. Always sharing it. Always taking care not to hurt anything. That's the way Willie lived his life.

One night Willie gave a snowflake lecture in town. There wasn't an empty chair in the room. In the middle of the lecture, he walked over to the window and stared at the sky. Then he slipped on his coat and walked out.

After the door closed, people peeked through the frost on the windows.

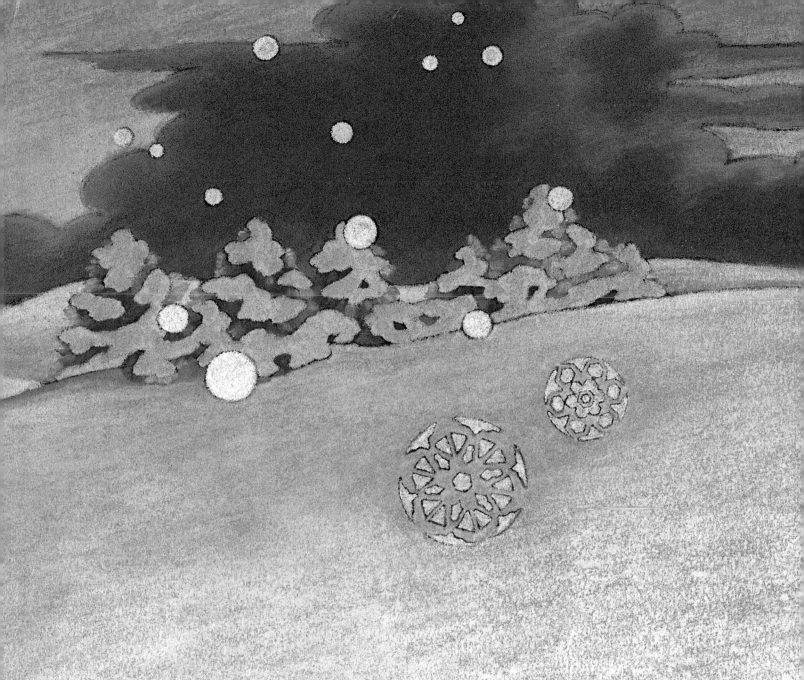

There was Willie, heading for home.

"I'm not surprised," someone in the crowd said with a chuckle. "It's starting to snow." By the time Willie walked the six miles home, the storm became a blizzard.

Next morning, Willie woke with a bad cold. It turned into pneumonia.

Two days before Christmas, my brother died. Snowflakes were filling the sky.

I bet they were saying good-bye.

"He saw something in the snowflakes which other men failed to see, not because they could not see, but because they had not the patience to look."

—From "Bentley's Contribution,"
Burlington Free Press,
Burlington, Vermont,
December 24,1931

Author's Note

Wilson A. Bentley (1865–1931) was a Vermont dairy farmer, a writer, a musician, and a self-taught scientist.

During his lifetime, he took 5,381 photomicrographs (photographs taken through a microscope) of snow and ice crystals. More than 2,500 of his pictures appeared in the book *Snow Crystals*, published in 1931.

Bentley also studied rain, clouds, auroras, and weather patterns. Between 1898 and 1904, he measured the size of 344 raindrops from 70 different storms.

His work helped people around the world understand that every snowflake is as individual—and as beautiful—as anything found in nature. Today, a plaque in his hometown of Jericho, Vermont, commemorates the life of Snowflake Bentley.

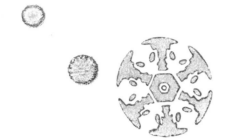
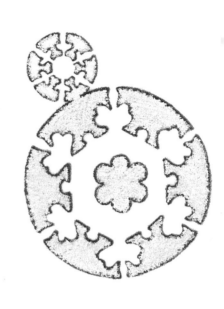

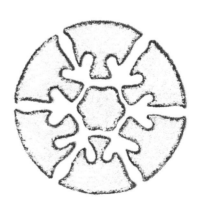

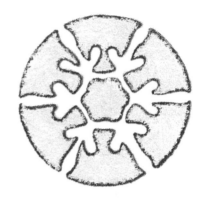

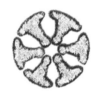

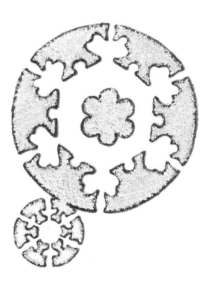